PHONICS

Fix that Sink!

Practising CVCC and
CCVC plus polysyllabic words

First published in 2007 by
Franklin Watts
338 Euston Road
London
NW1 3BH

Franklin Watts Australia
Level 17/207 Kent Street
Sydney
NSW 2000

A CIP catalogue record for this book is available
from the British Library.

ISBN: 978 0 7496 7131 0 (hbk)
ISBN: 978 0 7496 7318 5 (pbk)

Series Editor: Jackie Hamley
Series Advisors: Dr Barrie Wade, Dr Hilary Minns
Series Designer: Peter Scoulding

Printed in China

Franklin Watts is a division of
Hachette Children's Books.

READING CORNER

PHONICS

Fix that Sink!

by
Anne Adeney

Illustrated by
Charlie Fowkes

W
FRANKLIN WATTS
LONDON • SYDNEY

Anne Adeney
"This is for my lovely husband Richard. He is the original 'Plumbing Disaster Dad' and has flooded our house many times!"

Charlie Fowkes
"I would like to think I am good at fixing things. I especially like fixing my old beetle car."

Drip! Drip!
Splash! Splash!

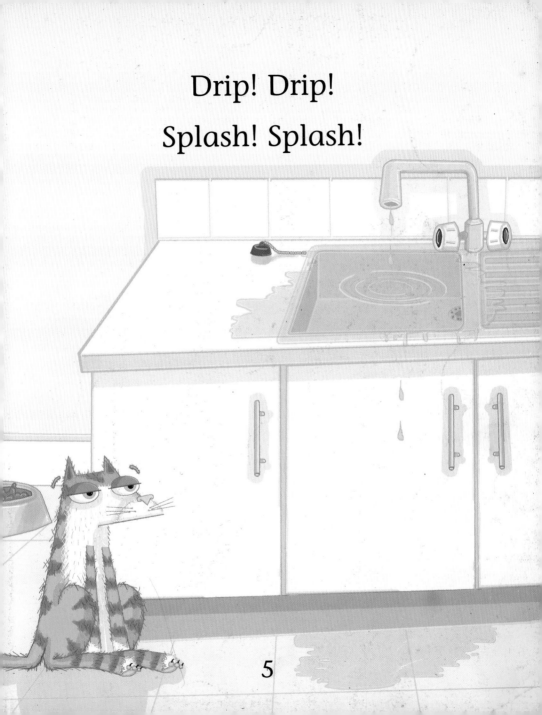

"We must fix that sink!"
said Mum.

"Ring ring"

6

"*I* will fix it!" said Dad.

8.

Dad got his belt and all the stuff from the chest.

"Can I help you fix
the sink?" said Jill.

13

"Yes, but you *must not* drop my stuff if you are helping, Jill!" said Dad.

"It must be a block in this bend," said Dad.

17

"I will twist it off to get at the block," said Dad.

CRACK!

Such a stink!

20

"Let me brush that off!" said Jill.

21

"You *must* get the plug back in
when I fix the bend," said Dad.

Next Dad did the tap.

"This is sticking," said Dad.

"I cannot twist it off."

CRASH!

Jill can splash in the pond.

Can you fix my sink?

But Dad cannot fix the sink!

Notes for parents and teachers.

READING CORNER PHONICS has been structured to provide maximum support for children learning to read through synthetic phonics. The stories are designed for independent reading but may also be used by adults for sharing with young children.

The teaching of early reading through synthetic phonics focuses on the 44 sounds in the English language, and how these sounds correspond to their written form in the 26 letters of the alphabet. Carefully controlled vocabulary makes these books accessible for children at different stages of phonics teaching, progressing from simple CVC (consonant-vowel-consonant) words such as "top" (t-o-p) to trisyllabic words such as "messenger" (mess-en-ger). READING CORNER PHONICS allows children to read words in context, and also provides visual clues and repetition to further support their reading. These books will help develop the all important confidence in the new reader, and encourage a love of reading that will last a lifetime!

If you are reading this book with a child, here are a few tips:

1. Talk about the story before you start reading. Look at the cover and the title. What might the story be about? Why might the child like it?

2. Encourage the child to reread the story, and to retell the story in their own words, using the illustrations to remind them what has happened.

3. Discuss the story and see if the child can relate it to their own experience, or perhaps compare it to another story they know.

4. Give praise! Small mistakes need not always be corrected. If a child is stuck on a word, ask them to try and sound it out and then blend it together again, or model this yourself. For example "wish" w-i-sh "wish".

READING CORNER PHONICS covers two grades of synthetic phonics teaching, with three levels at each grade. Each level has a certain number of words per story, indicated by the number of bars on the spine of the book:

GRADE 1		GRADE 2	
50 words	CVC words with short vowel sounds	130 words	CVCC and CCVC plus polysyllabic words
70 words	CVC words plus sounds of more than one letter	160 words	Long vowel sounds, CVCC and CCVC and polysyllabic words
100 words	Sounds of more than one letter, simple polysyllabic words	200 words	Long vowel sounds, trisyllabic words, tricky words